Caring for
Animals

Courtney was very excited. Barbie was letting her
spend the day at the Veterinary Surgery where
she worked as a vet. Courtney thought she
might be a vet too, when she grew up.

"How did you know you wanted to be a vet?"
Courtney asked Barbie.

"Well, I've always loved animals," said Barbie. "When
I was about your age, I had a kitten called Cuddles.
She was my very first pet and when I looked after
her, I think I knew that I wanted to be a vet."

When they arrived at the surgery, Courtney
was amazed to see all sorts of animals waiting
to see Barbie.
"Being a vet must be like having dozens of pets!"
said Courtney in amazement.
"In a way," said Barbie. "But the animals who come
to visit me only stay here until they're well again."

Just then, Megan hurried into the waiting room carrying
a cardboard box with a beautiful black cat inside.
"Barbie!" she cried. "I'm really worried about Midnight.
She's been meowing a lot and her stomach seems
swollen. Is she okay?"

Barbie led Megan and Courtney quickly into her examining room. She gently lifted Midnight out of the box and put her on the table. Courtney and Megan watched as Barbie examined the cat.

"Don't worry, Megan," said Barbie with a smile.
"I think I know what's wrong with Midnight. Leave
her here with me and come back for her at midday."
Courtney and Megan were surprised. Why was Barbie
smiling and telling Megan not to worry?

Barbie's next patient was a dog called Rascal. He barked happily and wagged his tail when he saw her. "It's nice to see you, too!" laughed Barbie, stroking his head.
"Rascal doesn't look ill to me," said Courtney.

"Not all my patients are ill," said Barbie. "Just like
people, animals need regular check-ups to stay healthy."
Barbie gave Rascal his vaccinations.
"I had injections before I started school," said Courtney.
"Just like Rascal!" said Barbie.

Barbie saw a few more animals and then picked up her medical kit and headed for the door.

"Come on, Courtney," she said.

"Do I have to go home already?" said Courtney, sadly.

"Of course not!" laughed Barbie. "We're going to visit some patients who can't come to the surgery."
"Oh, no! Are they too ill to get here?" asked Courtney in concern.
"No, they're not too ill, just too big!" said Barbie.

Barbie drove them to a nearby farm.
"Oh! We're going to see horses!" said Courtney.
The farm's owner, Mr Greene, watched as his daughter,
Ashley, led a pony out of the barn.

"Stardancer cut her face when she tried to open her stall," said Ashley.

Barbie examined Stardancer's face. "It's not a serious cut," said Barbie. "But you do need to keep the cut clean until it heals," Barbie told Stardancer softly.

"How will Stardancer wash her face?" asked Courtney.

"Well, I do have a little trick," said Barbie.
She filled a bucket with clean water and floated
some apples in it.
"Stardancer loves apples!" said Ashley.

Stardancer rushed towards the bucket and happily
dunked her face into it to pick out the apples.
She didn't realise she was keeping her cut clean
as well as having a tasty treat!

Barbie and Courtney drove back to the surgery.
Suddenly, Barbie slammed on the brakes. A puppy
had run into the road, straight in front of her car!
Barbie checked the puppy. It was fine, but Barbie
went to speak to its owner.

"It is very important that you keep your puppy
on a lead," she said, "especially as he hasn't learnt
to obey your commands."
The boy listened carefully, promising to keep his
puppy on a lead and train it properly.

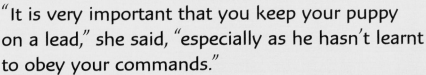

Back at the surgery, Barbie checked the animals
staying in the kennels.
"Some animals have to stay here overnight, or for a
few days to get better," Barbie explained to Courtney.

"If they have been very poorly, we keep them here and check on their progress. When they are well enough to go home, their owners come and collect them."
"It's just like being in hospital!" said Courtney.

When Barbie walked into the waiting room,
Megan rushed up to her.
"Oh, Barbie, I've been so worried about Midnight!"
she cried. "Have you managed to make her well, again?"

"Don't worry, Megan," said Barbie softly. "Midnight is feeling much better now. Come on through, and you'll see she has a surprise for you!"

Megan and Courtney tiptoed into the room.
They both gasped in surprise.
"She's had kittens!" exclaimed Megan, looking at
Midnight lying in a basket with her new kittens.

"How many kittens has she had?" asked Courtney.
Megan counted. "There are five!" she said.
"Thank you so much, Barbie!"

"The new kittens have to stay with Midnight for at least six weeks," said Barbie and she carefully explained to Megan and Courtney how to look after the new born kittens.

Courtney smiled. She had enjoyed her time with Barbie and she now knew for sure that she would be a vet when she grew up!

This edition published in Great Britain 2002
by Egmont Books Limited
239 Kensington High Street, London W8 6SA
First published in Great Britain 1999 by Egmont Books Limited
Originally published in the USA by Golden Books Limited
as 'A Day with the Pet Doctor' by Katherine Poindexter, 1998.
ISBN 1 4052 01541
1 3 5 7 9 10 8 6 4 2
Printed in China.